The Secret Mermaid

Underwater Magic

Sue Mongredien

Illustrated by Maria Pearson

USBORNE

For Holly Powell,
with lots of love from Mum.

First published in the UK in 2009 by Usborne Publishing Ltd., Usborne House,
83-85 Saffron Hill, London EC1N 8RT, England. www.usborne.com

Copyright © Sue Mongredien Ltd., 2009
Illustrations copyright © Usborne Publishing Ltd., 2009

The right of Sue Mongredien to be identified as the author of this work has been asserted
by her in accordance with the Copyright, Designs and Patents Act, 1988.

The name Usborne and the devices ♛ ⊕ are Trade Marks of Usborne Publishing Ltd.

A CIP catalogue record for this book is available from the British Library.
This edition published in America in 2016 AE.
PB ISBN 9780794534882   ALB ISBN 9781601303738
JFMAMJJASO   D/17   01525-10
Printed in China.

Contents

Molly

Ella

Delphi

Shivana

Undersea Kingdom

Coral

Queen Luna

Princess Silva

Pearl

Chapter One

Molly Holmes jumped as rain suddenly lashed against the cottage window. She got up from the saggy old sofa in the living room to peer outside. It was early evening in midsummer, but already the sky was dark and bruised-looking, with dense gray and purple clouds. Raindrops pattered against the glass, sliding down it in long, glistening trails.

Her gran came to join her at the window.

"I don't think anyone will be taking a stroll
along Horseshoe Bay this evening," Gran joked,
slipping an arm around Molly.

"Nor swimming," Molly replied with a smile. The sea looked as dark and menacing as the sky, and huge white-crested waves were rolling in, crashing onto the sand. She shivered as she thought about how cold the damp sand would feel on bare skin.

"It's not the nicest evening, is it?" Molly's mom commented, coming to stand next to them with Toby, Molly's baby brother, in her arms. Toby had bright red spots on his cheeks and tears were spouting from his eyes. He kept putting his fingers in his mouth and crying. "All right, sweet pea," Molly's mom said, rocking him back and forth. "He's got his first tooth coming through," she explained to Molly. "I think we're probably in for a noisy night from this little man."

Molly's dad came in from the kitchen just then, carrying a tray laden with mugs of steaming hot chocolate and a plate of ginger snaps.

He set the tray down, then glanced over at the fireplace, which hadn't been lit while Molly's family had been living in the cottage. "I'll go out to the shed and chop a few logs to make a fire soon," he said. "It doesn't feel like summer anymore."

"Still, it could be worse," Molly's mom said, rocking Toby. "We could be out at sea. Imagine that, on a night like tonight! Thank goodness we'll be cozy and warm here instead."

Molly smiled to herself, not daring to reply. In truth, she hoped she *would* be at sea tonight – with her new mermaid friends!

Since Molly's family had moved in with her gran, Molly had discovered a wonderful secret. Sometimes, at night, she transformed into a mermaid – the new "secret mermaid," one of six special mermaid Shell-Keepers, just like her gran had been before her.

The Shell-Keeper
mermaids all had
fragments of the
same magical conch
shell; Gran had given
Molly her creamy-
white piece on a silver
chain the day Molly's
family had moved in. Molly hadn't

realized just how amazing a present it was until
that first night, when bright pink sparkles had
flooded out from the shell, and the mermaid
magic had begun, whisking Molly to the ocean
for an adventure she'd never forget!

Unfortunately, Molly had discovered from the
other Shell-Keepers that a bad mermaid known
as Carlotta the Dark Queen had stolen the other
five pieces of conch to use for her own wicked
ends. And, as the secret mermaid, Molly had to

help the other mermaids find them again. She'd already helped her friend Ella get her piece back, but there were still four fragments of conch missing – and Molly was desperate to return to the ocean and seek them out.

It was frustrating, Molly thought, that she couldn't just turn herself into a mermaid whenever she wanted to. She had to wait for the magic to come all on its own. But it did mean that she looked forward to going up to bed each night – she was always hopeful of another mermaid adventure!

She turned away from the storm outside the window. "I'll just go and get my pajamas on," she told her parents, and Gran gave her a smile. Molly smiled back and went out of the room and up the narrow stairs. She would have loved to know more about Gran's adventures as a secret mermaid all those years ago, but she knew that Gran was forbidden to talk to anyone about them – just as she, Molly, had promised to keep quiet about the mermaids too. Somehow it made it all the more exciting, though, hugging such an amazing secret to herself.

When she'd said goodnight to her parents and Gran, she got into bed, and reached out to pick up her special shell. It felt cool and smooth in her palm, and she closed her eyes with a wistful smile. "I hope I can help you soon, mermaids," she murmured.

It took a long time for Molly to drift off that night. She tossed and turned in bed, but she kept hearing her brother's plaintive cries of pain from his bedroom next door. The storm was still raging outside too, with rain spattering against the window. Molly could hear the roar of the waves from her bed as they thundered against the rocks.

After a while, Molly opened her eyes. "I'm never going to get to sleep," she muttered to herself. But as she said the words, her conch began to glow with its magical pink light, and a mist of tiny golden sparkles appeared around the shell. "Oh!" gasped Molly in excitement and she shut her eyes at once. The mermaid magic was beginning again!

Chapter Two

Molly had been a mermaid twice before now, but she still wasn't used to the peculiar melting sensation as her body transformed. Her legs in particular felt as if they were dissolving into nothing – it was rather alarming! But then, suddenly, she could feel the coolness of seawater against her skin and she opened her eyes eagerly. Yes! She was a mermaid again. Her legs had vanished, and now she had her very own shimmering silver tail flicking behind her!

"Hello, Molly," came a voice from nearby. "I thought that was you!"

Molly turned to see Delphi, one of the other Shell-Keeper mermaids. Delphi had bobbed auburn hair, green eyes and a sprinkling of freckles over her nose. She wore a jade-green top, and had a pale green flower tucked in her hair.

"Hello!" Molly cried joyfully and swam over toward her. Something felt different though. Why was it so hard to swim all of a sudden? Usually, as a mermaid, Molly could speed through the water very fast.

Delphi noticed Molly struggle and came to meet her halfway. "The current is really strong today, isn't it?" she said. She hugged Molly in welcome. "There have been some terrible storms lately, too. Usually, my piece of the conch helps me protect sailors at sea – I can use its powers to guide their ships safely back to harbor. But without it, I haven't been able to do anything, and there have almost been some dreadful shipwrecks."

"Well, I can help you look for your shell," Molly said at once. "I—"

Before she could finish her sentence, though, a pod of dolphins had appeared, smiling as they dove down through the water toward the two mermaids.

"Ahh," Delphi murmured to Molly. "Here come my little helpers. Or rather, they *think* they're helping."

The first dolphin to reach them made some excited whistling, snickering noises to Delphi, its eyes bright and alert. Molly couldn't take her eyes off the beautiful creature. She could hardly believe she was so close to it!

"You think you've found the shell?" Delphi replied. "Okay, we'll follow you. Come on, Molly, let's see what they've got this time."

She flicked her tail fin and surged away through the water. Molly gave her own tail a sharp wiggle and swam after her. She was surprised that Delphi didn't seem more enthusiastic at the dolphin's message. "What's up?" she hissed to her as they followed the sleek, silvery dolphins.

Delphi gave a tired smile in reply. "I do love

the dolphins – they're so cheerful and bouncy and eager to help," she said in a low voice, "but they're a bit *too* eager to help, if you know what I mean. They've been in and out of the shipwrecks looking for my conch piece, and they keep thinking they've seen it, and coming to get me, when really it's just another piece of human treasure that they've discovered." She rolled her eyes comically. "What with them, and Princess Silva hanging around all the time asking if I've found the shell yet, I've hardly had a minute to myself."

Molly bit her lip, hoping she would be more help than the dolphins and Princess Silva. Maybe Delphi didn't even *want* her hanging around – maybe she was secretly wishing Molly hadn't turned up at all!

Delphi caught the doubtful expression on Molly's face and put a hand on her arm.

"Oh – I didn't mean I wanted to be on my own *now*!" she said quickly. "I heard how wonderful you were at helping Ella when she'd been thrown onto the sand by that scary killer whale. I'm really happy you're here to help me, too – truly, Molly!"

Molly smiled in relief. "Oh good," she said. "I'm happy to be here."

They swam on, and Molly remembered Delphi's earlier comment about Princess Silva, daughter of the Merqueen. Queen Luna was lovely, but there was something a little strange about the princess, Molly thought privately. She always seemed to be hanging around in the background, listening and watching without saying very much. Maybe she was just shy, though.

The dolphins had stopped before a huge rock on the seabed and were pointing their shiny noses at it, all making whistling noises at once.

"Okay, let's have a look," Delphi said in a good-humored way. Molly could tell she didn't really believe her shell would be there.

But then Delphi's mouth fell open in surprise and her eyes lit up. "Oh! My conch! You really *did* find it!" she cried, and she threw her arms around the nearest dolphin, covering his head with happy kisses.

Molly swam over to the rock excitedly for a closer look. Sure enough, wedged into a crevice was Delphi's piece of the conch! The shell's creamy surface seemed to glow against the dark, barnacle-covered rock, and was half-hidden by a spiky round object that rested on top of it. Was the spiky thing some kind of plant? Molly wondered.

Delphi patted the other dolphins lovingly, then joined Molly in front of the rock. "At last!" she cried happily, reaching out a hand to move the spiky thing. "Oh, I've been so worried! And now—"

"Hey!" the spiky thing snapped in a bad-tempered way, making Molly jump back in alarm. "Get your hand away from me, or I'll jab you with my spines!"

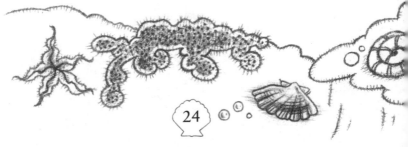

Molly stared at the spiky thing and then questioningly at Delphi. "What *is* that?" she whispered.

"It's a sea urchin," Delphi replied in a low voice. "A grumpy sea urchin at that!"

She turned back to the creature. "But you're on my shell," she said to it politely. "Please would you move, so that I can get it?"

"No," the sea urchin told her. "It's mine now, I found it. Lovely and smooth it is, too, after that craggy old rock. Shouldn't have been so careless with it, should you?"

"Oh please," Molly put in. "It was stolen from her – she wasn't being careless!"

The sea urchin's red spines rippled in the current. They did look horribly sharp, Molly thought to herself. "I said no, and I mean no!" the sea urchin replied crossly. "And if either of you comes anywhere near me again, I'll jab you so hard, you'll be sorry!"

Chapter Three

Molly and Delphi looked at one another, then swam a little way away from the bad-tempered sea urchin. "A sea urchin's spines aren't poisonous, but they are painful and difficult to get out," Delphi said to Molly with a sigh. "And it means what it says too, I'm sure."

"Well, we'll just have to think of a way we can persuade it to move," Molly said, racking her brains for an idea. "And before the Dark

Queen finds out your conch is here, too."
Then the sea urchin's words came back to her.
"Lovely and smooth" it had called the shell.
So maybe if they could find something else
that was lovely and smooth, they might be
able to talk the sea urchin into trading…

Molly whispered her idea to Delphi, who
clapped her hands. "Yes – that might just
work," she said. "Come on, let's see what the
old grouch thinks."

The two mermaids swam back to the
sea urchin, which
waggled its spines
threateningly
when it
sensed them
approaching.
"Now what?"
it asked sharply.

"I was just wondering," Molly said in her politest voice, "how you felt about trading that old shell for something even better?"

"Something sparkly, perhaps," Delphi said coaxingly. "Your spines would look really good then, wouldn't they?"

The sea urchin hesitated. "What sort of sparkly thing?" it asked in a gruff voice.

"Treasure," Delphi told it. "I found some lovely pieces earlier. Smooth, shiny silver plates...some golden goblets you could make a cave out of... What do you think?"

There was an agonizing pause while the sea urchin considered this. Then it spoke. "Very well, then," it said. "But no trickery!"

"No trickery," Molly promised solemnly. "Come on, Delphi, let's go on a treasure hunt."

The two mermaids swam away quickly, pleased that the sea urchin was being more reasonable.

Now they just had to find some treasure!

"I know the perfect place," Delphi told Molly. "There's a shipwreck not far from here. The dolphins were exploring it earlier; there are all sorts of treasures and trinkets there."

The mermaids swam on, and Molly's own piece of conch bobbed around on its chain. Her conch had already worked some powerful magic when she'd asked for its help in the past, and Molly was glad to have it with her.

The sea was still very hard to swim through. The current was stronger than ever, and Molly felt herself buffeted backward by it, despite her muscular tail. "It's another storm," Delphi said anxiously, gazing up above them. "I can hear the rain from all the way down here."

"What's that?" Molly asked, seeing a huge dark object in the distance. "Is it some kind of ship?"

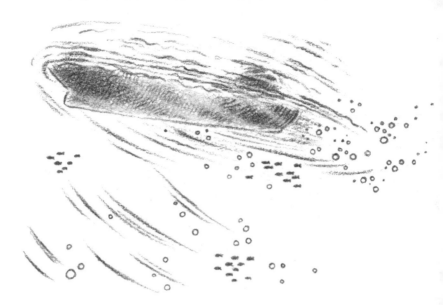

Delphi peered through the raging current.
"It's an oil tanker," she said after a moment,
and a look of horror crossed her face.

"What's it doing up there? It should be further out – there's a rocky outcrop not far from here."

Molly felt worried. She knew that an oil spill would mean disaster for the marine environment. "Do you think the tanker might hit the rocks?"

"Yes, if we can't get it back on course," Delphi replied, her mouth in a tense line. "Oh, we must get my conch quickly! Then I'll be able to quell the storm and guide the tanker back where it should be!"

"Come on," Molly said. "Let's grab some treasure for the sea urchin fast."

She and Delphi swam as hard as they could until they reached the shipwreck. The boat was wooden and very old, and lay at an angle, battered and broken on the seabed, with fish swimming in and out of the holes in its sides. There were still the remains of a mast and crossbeam standing, and even some of the old rigging floating from the beams.

Delphi dove through a gap in the ship's wrecked hull and Molly followed her, taking care to avoid the jagged edges.

Inside the main part of the ship, it was eerie and still. Molly couldn't help thinking about all the people who'd been on board when the ship had gone down. Now the wreck was home to starfish and sea anemones. Seaweed grew through the holes, the fronds swaying over the aged wood. But she wasn't here to sightsee, Molly reminded herself, as a vision of the oil tanker flashed into her mind. She and Delphi needed to find some treasure for the sea urchin – and quickly!

Molly saw a gleam of silver, half-buried beneath a large clump of bobbly seaweed and some fine pale sand, and dug away with her fingers to uncover a small silver dish. "I've found this!" she shouted to Delphi, holding it up. "What do you think?"

"Great, I'll put it in my bag," said Delphi, from further inside the ship. "Let's just open this chest and see what's inside too. We should take a few things with us in case that grouchy sea urchin doesn't like what we offer him. There might be something even better in here."

Molly saw that her friend was scrabbling to pry open an old metal chest which was tarnished and dented with age.

Molly swam over and helped lift the rusted catch, using a mussel shell as a lever. "There!" she said, panting as the lid finally swung up with a creak.

"Ooh," Delphi said, peering inside.

"Doubloons! Pirate gold!"

Molly reached in and took out a handful of the old coins, still gleaming gold after all their time underwater. "The chest must have been pretty watertight," she said. "They seem good as new!"

"Oh, and look what's underneath them," Delphi said, burrowing into the bright mound of coins. She held up a curved knife with a jeweled handle.

"A cutlass! This really must have been a pirate ship once upon a time." She ran a finger along the blade of the cutlass and shivered. "I think we'll leave that here, though," she said. She gathered up a handful of coins instead and slipped them, along with a ruby-studded golden goblet and the silver dish, into the little green bag she wore around one shoulder. "There. That'll do. Let's go!"

Molly closed the chest again, and followed Delphi up through a hole overhead. But as she swam back over the old deck of the shipwreck, she caught sight of a pair of red eyes glowing through the murky water ahead and her heart lurched with fear. Oh, no. The last time she'd seen a sea creature with eyes like that it had been enchanted by the Dark Queen Carlotta, and it had attacked Ella! Was it the killer whale again, come back to try to see off Molly and Delphi this time?

"Delphi!" Molly hissed, her voice coming out shaky and frightened. "Delphi, look! I think the Dark Queen's killer whale is coming for us!"

Delphi flicked her head around to see, and a look of terror crossed her face. "That's no killer whale," she said. "It's a shark, Molly. A great white shark!"

Chapter Four

Molly was terrified. She knew that the great white shark was one of the deadliest creatures in the ocean. And if those red eyes were anything to go by, it was one of the Dark Queen's servants as well, like the killer whale had been. She and Delphi were in serious trouble!

The shark was swimming toward the wreck at great speed now, and the two frightened mermaids looked at one another.

"It could out-swim us any day," Delphi said shakily. "Our only hope is your conch, Molly. Can you think of a way it could help us get rid of the shark?"

Molly was so frightened, her mind went blank at Delphi's question. But after a few moments, she remembered the cutlass. That sharp, shiny cutlass. She didn't want to hurt the shark, of course – she wouldn't hurt any ocean creature – but there might be something she could do with the cutlass to see it off...if she could only think!

She dodged to the bottom of the wreck and fumbled to open the chest again, then grabbed the jeweled cutlass handle, her fingers shaking. It felt heavy and solid in her grasp as she quickly returned to Delphi's side. Then, as the shark swam toward the mast, an idea finally came to her. She gripped her conch with her free hand and cried out, "Conch! Help me cut through wood!"

The conch glowed with a bright pink light for a moment, and so did the cutlass, its jewels sparkling and glittering through the murky water. Then, holding her breath and praying this would work, Molly swung the cutlass blade at the mast with all her might.

"Go for it, Molly!" Delphi called out.

Molly was braced for the cutlass to bounce back uselessly – she'd seen her dad sawing logs before and knew that cutting through wood was hard work. But the cutlass sliced through the old oak mast as easily as a hot knife through butter.

The top part of the mast teetered where it had been cut, and Delphi shoved it forcefully in the shark's direction. *Crash!* Down it fell, with the crossbeams toppling to the seabed, neatly trapping the shark in the rigging.

The angry shark bit at the rigging with its sharp teeth, its red eyes furious. Molly felt faint at the sight of all those rows of curving, vicious teeth inside the mighty creature's jaws, but it couldn't seem to free itself.

"Nice work!" Delphi cried, throwing her arms around Molly. "Let's go back to the sea urchin, quick. We need to get my conch so I can stop that oil tanker!"

"Will the shark be all right?" Molly asked uncertainly. Even though it was a scary creature, she didn't want it to come to any harm.

"It'll be fine," Delphi assured her. "It's not hurt. Sooner or later, it'll chomp its way through the ropes. But by then, we'll be long gone. Come on!"

Delphi grabbed Molly's hand and the two mermaids swam back toward the sea urchin. "I hope we won't be too late," Molly said. "What if the Dark Queen gets to it before us?"

"Don't say that," Delphi begged. "We *must* get my shell. Look – there's the oil tanker – and it's even closer to the rocks now." Her face was pale. "If the oil is spilled, it will kill so many of our creatures – birds, fish, even dolphins and seals – by poisoning them or covering them in the sticky oil. We've got to stop it with my conch piece, Molly. We've just got to!" she said desperately, swimming faster than ever.

Delphi looked almost sick with worry, and Molly felt she had to take charge. "Come on, let's hurry on to the sea urchin, then," she said. "And if he's still being difficult, I'll just grab him off your shell. I don't care about a few spikes!" she added, trying to sound brave. Really, though, she was nervous. The sea urchin had such sharp-looking spines, it would be like picking up an aggressive hedgehog. But she'd have to do it now, however much it hurt. They had to save that oil tanker from crashing!

The two mermaids reached the craggy rock where the sea urchin had made its home and – thank goodness! – Delphi's shell was still visible beneath it. Molly took the silver dish from Delphi's bag and held it out temptingly to the spiky little creature. "Here you go," she said in her most coaxing voice. "Do you want to try this for size?"

The sea urchin hesitated for a moment, and Molly held her breath. *Please!* she willed it in her head. *Please just move!*

"Go on, it's really beautiful," she urged. "I bet your spines will look extra-bright on it." Still there was no movement from the sea urchin. Was it just being obstinate?

She was about to try one last time to persuade it when she suddenly saw its spines twitch. And then, one by one, they all began rotating, pushing the sea urchin along the rock at quite a rapid speed. Molly and Delphi exchanged hopeful glances as the sea urchin, spines rippling, propelled itself off the shell and onto the silver dish.

Delphi's hand hovered near her shell. "Well?" she asked, rather impatiently. "Is that all right?"

The sea urchin gave a contented sort of wiggle on the silver. "Very nice," it said in a pleased-sounding voice. "Very comfortable."

Molly let her breath out in a great rush of
relief. "Fantastic," she said, setting the dish
down on the seabed. "And your spines do look
wonderful against the silver."

Delphi grinned at Molly and stretched out an
arm for her conch shell. "So I'll take this now,
thanks very much!"

"Oh, of course," the sea urchin said. "Please
take it away. Not half as nice as my new dish."

Delphi was hardly listening, though. As she tugged at her conch piece in the rock crevice, it glowed a bright gold. Molly's shell was shining with light too, and she held it tightly, remembering that its magic had helped Ella retrieve her shell from the underwater cave.

"Oh yes!" cheered Delphi, as her shell came away smoothly in her hand, shining with an even brighter golden light. Sparks shot out from all around it, lighting up trails in the water as far as the eye could see. It almost looked like a firework in Delphi's cupped hands, Molly thought, her eyes dazzled by the sight.

"Oh, it's good to have this back," Delphi said happily. She lifted it to her cheek and pressed it against her face. "And now we must use its magic to stop the oil tanker. Come on, Molly. We need to get as close as we can!"

Molly hastened after her friend, whose silver tail was already pushing her through the sea like a glittering torpedo. "The current isn't so strong now," Molly shouted as they swam.

Delphi looked back over her shoulder with a faint smile. "The magic of my conch is working right again, now it's back with me," she said. "It's made the current calmer, so it should be easier for us to guide the oil tanker away from the rocks. Let's just hope we can get to it in time!"

But as she spoke, there was a terrible sound of scraping metal in the distance. The mermaids peered anxiously ahead to see the bottom of the oil tanker dragging against the rocks.

"Oh no!" Delphi cried in horror. "We're too late!"

Chapter Five

"What should we do?" cried Molly.

"We'll have to turn the direction of the current so that we can push the tanker off the rocks," Delphi said decisively, and grabbed Molly's hand. "The magic is more powerful if we join together," she said. "Hold your conch and concentrate!"

Molly did as she was told, gripping her conch with her free hand until pink sparkly magic spiraled through her fingers.

"By the power of the conch, turn the current!" Delphi cried out. Magic crackled from her shell too, but the oil tanker didn't move. "Again," she said to Molly. "Let's say it together."

Molly held her conch, willing the magic to work with all her energy. "By the power of the conch, turn the current!" the two mermaids shouted as one.

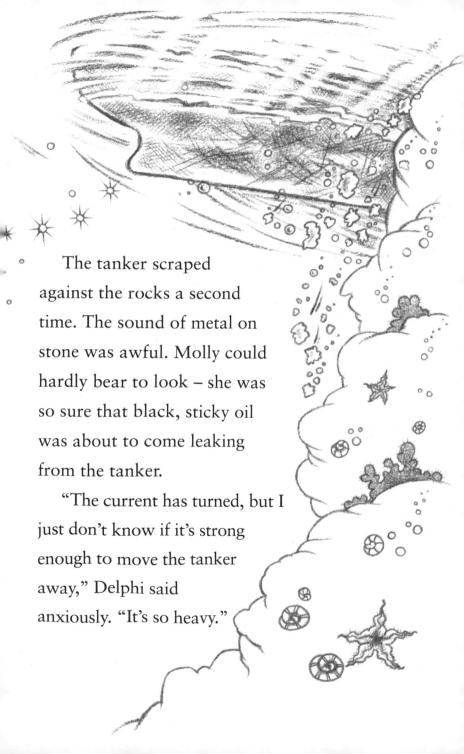

The tanker scraped against the rocks a second time. The sound of metal on stone was awful. Molly could hardly bear to look – she was so sure that black, sticky oil was about to come leaking from the tanker.

"The current has turned, but I just don't know if it's strong enough to move the tanker away," Delphi said anxiously. "It's so heavy."

"Is there anything else that could move it?" Molly wondered aloud. She remembered how she'd levered up the lid of the treasure chest with a mussel shell. "Maybe if we could find something to push it along? I'm not sure what though..."

Delphi snapped her fingers suddenly, her eyes bright. "A friendly whale!" she said. "One of the humpbacks would help us, I'm sure." She put her

forefinger and thumb into her mouth and blew a series of piercing whistles. Then she scanned the water hopefully. "If any of the humpback whales are around, they should come to my call," she said.

Molly couldn't help thinking about the scary killer whale she and Ella had encountered. She really hoped the humpback whales hadn't been recruited to the Dark Queen's army too. They certainly didn't need another red-eyed creature to attack them now!

But Delphi put a hand to her ear. "Listen!" she said. "They're coming. Can you hear them?"

Molly listened – and her fears were forgotten as she heard beautiful singing noises, mournful and melodic, sweeping up to high notes and down to low moaning sounds. "Is that really the whales?" she asked in surprise. She had no idea whales could make such music.

Delphi nodded. "Beautiful, isn't it?" she said. "Look, here they come now. It's a whole pod – fantastic!"

In the distance, Molly could see a group of gray, white and black specks that grew larger as they approached. She could make out their shapes now, and their huge speckled flippers that sent them effortlessly through the water. The singing grew louder and the sound sent shivers down Molly's spine. *I will never forget this*, she thought to herself in wonder.

Moments later, the pod of whales had reached the mermaids. It was quite something to have so many large creatures massing before you, Molly thought, feeling overwhelmed at their size. They were close enough now that she could see great scars and scratches on their skin, and barnacles crusted over their bodies. They all had throat grooves running from their chins to their bellies, and deep notches in their tails.

The whales fell silent as Delphi sang back to them. Molly guessed she was explaining the problem with the tanker, because all the whales suddenly turned toward its vast dark hull as it swayed in the water. Then, when Delphi had finished her last note, the pod of whales moved as one to the tanker and pushed at it with their mighty heads.

Molly gripped her conch again, not knowing what else to do. "By the power of the conch, help the whales," she murmured under her breath. She knew they were taking a risk, coming so close to the tanker that might at any moment start leaking toxic oil.

She could hardly bear to think about what the consequences could be – they were too awful.

Her conch glittered again and a flood of sparkly light shone out, streaking through the water around the whales. Molly watched anxiously as the whales pushed...and pushed...

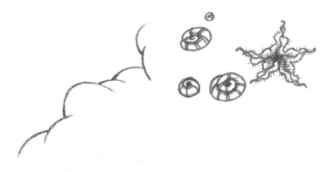

"It's moving!" Delphi cried. She was also holding her conch very tightly. "I'm sure it's moving!"

Molly stared. Delphi was right. Slowly, very slowly, the force of the whales combined with the current was shifting the oil tanker away from the rocks. The tanker settled in the water as the whales pushed and shoved at it, and then it began to drift away as the current caught it. A muffled cheer floated down through the water to them and Molly realized, for the first time, that there were sailors on board who must have been just as fearful as she and Delphi had been.

The whales kept on pushing the tanker along until it was a safe distance from the rocks. Then they backed off and watched it sail away.

Delphi threw her arms around Molly. "They did it!" she cried, her voice catching with relief.

"They were amazing," Molly said. "But so were you for thinking of asking them to help."

Delphi gave her a smile. "*We* did it," she said, correcting herself. "All together. What a team!"

The whales waited as the oil tanker began moving off in the opposite direction of its own accord. Then they turned, their bodies gleaming, and began jumping up through the water, their heads breaking the surface and returning with a slapping sound.

"What are they doing?" Molly asked, marveling at the whales' acrobatics.

Delphi smiled. "It's called breaching," she replied. "They're playing." She sang out to them in the special whale language and waved. "Thank you!" she called, smiling.

The whales waved their great long flippers back at the mermaids, and swam away, some of them still making graceful breaching movements, which sent ripples of water in their wake. Molly heard their haunting singing start up again as they went.

"Good old humpbacks," Delphi said fondly. "Wonderful creatures." She smiled at Molly. "Have you got enough energy to swim with me to the Undersea Kingdom?" she asked. "We must tell the Merqueen that we've found my conch, and that it's safe from the Dark Queen."

"Sure," Molly said, eager to visit the place where all the mermaids lived again. "I'd like to."

"Great," Delphi said. She slipped her conch into the pretty green bag she wore, and looked confused for a moment as she pulled something else out. It was one of the gold doubloons from the shipwreck. "Oh, I'd forgotten about these," she said. She pressed it into Molly's hand. "Here, you should have it," she said. "A souvenir from the pirate wreck!"

Molly stared in delight at the solid golden coin in her hand. Her fingers closed around it and she smiled gratefully at Delphi. "Thank you," she said.

"This has been such an exciting adventure!"

"Let's go and tell the Merqueen all about it," Delphi said. "Come on!"

Molly followed her friend through the water. It was so much easier to swim now that the storm had died down and the current wasn't so turbulent. It felt like no time before Molly could see the golden gates ahead, marking the entrance to the mermaids' kingdom.

Delphi took a small golden key from a pocket in her bag and unlocked the gates, then ushered Molly inside. She took Molly by the hand and led her through the kingdom toward the Merqueen's palace, a tall, grand building carved from white rock, with decorative towers and balconies.

Queen Luna must have been watching out for arrivals, for she swam through the mother-of-pearl palace doors to greet them almost at once, her dark blue cape billowing out behind her. Molly thought the Merqueen was one of the most beautiful beings she'd ever met, with her kindly eyes, and her chestnut hair coiled so regally on her head. The Merqueen was followed by her daughter, Princess Silva.

Delphi's face was wreathed in smiles as she greeted them. "We've got my piece of the conch!" she declared happily, taking it out of her green bag and holding it up in the air.

"Oh, my dears, that's splendid news!" Queen Luna cried, coming over and embracing first Delphi and then Molly. Over the Merqueen's shoulder, Molly could see Princess Silva's face – and was shocked to see the bitter twist of the young princess's mouth. Why wasn't Silva happy?

The princess seemed to feel Molly's eyes
upon her and started as she realized she was
being observed, quickly putting on a fake smile.
But Molly wasn't convinced. The smile didn't
reach the princess's dark eyes. Something was
wrong – but what?

Chapter Six

Delphi didn't seem to have noticed anything unusual about the princess; she was far too busy recounting their adventure to the Merqueen. "And Molly was amazing! She thought of this brilliant plan to stop the shark from attacking us – it had been enchanted by Carlotta, I'm sure, because it had the spookiest red eyes – and then we called the humpbacks to help us stop an oil tanker from crashing, and…"

Molly looked toward the princess again, but she was swimming back into the palace. *Strange,* she thought to herself. *I hope she's all right.*

Queen Luna was smiling as the words tumbled breathlessly out of Delphi's mouth. "Well done, both of you," she said. "It's really wonderful to have three pieces of the conch safe from the Dark Queen. Let's hope Pearl, Coral and Shivana can bring us good news soon, too. Molly, once again, you've been a great help. Thank you, my dear."

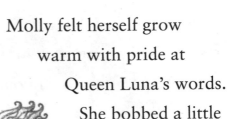

Molly felt herself grow
warm with pride at
Queen Luna's words.
She bobbed a little
curtsy, blushing.
"You're welcome,
Your Majesty,"
she said. "I'm just
glad I could help."
"You certainly
did that." Queen
Luna smiled. "And
now it's time for you
to return to your own
world, secret mermaid.
Dawn is breaking."

"But—" Molly put in. She hated being sent
back home – especially when there were still three
other pieces of the conch left to find!

The Merqueen put her hands gently on Molly's shoulders. "We will see you again soon, I promise," she said. "But for now... farewell."

"Goodbye," Molly said, a little sadly. She hugged Delphi one last time and dropped into another curtsy before the queen. Then she was surrounded by electric-blue sparkles of mermaid magic and felt as if she were being pulled very fast to the surface of the water, with the Undersea Kingdom blurring before her eyes.

The next thing she knew was the feeling of sunlight on her face through a gap in the curtains. She rubbed her eyes and sat up to see a shaft of white morning light on her bedroom floor. The sight was enough to make her scramble out of bed at once – a sunny day, after all the storms they'd had recently! – but as she moved, she realized she was holding something.

She uncurled her fingers to see a gold coin in her palm…and the adventures of the night before came rushing back into her mind. A pirate doubloon from the shipwreck! Oh, it had been so exciting! Way better than any dream she could have had.

She went to the window and stared out at the sea. It looked flat and smooth now, sparkling a glorious blue in the early morning sunlight.

Perfect weather for going down to the beach,
she thought to herself with a happy stretch.

Molly couldn't stop smiling as she put on her
bathrobe, and all but skipped down to the
breakfast table.

"Hello, Molly," her mom said, pouring her
a glass of orange juice. "Have you seen what
Toby's got this morning?"

Molly turned to look at her baby brother,
who was sitting in his high chair, banging a
plastic spoon on the tray and grinning. There,
on his lower gum, was a single white tooth, just
peeking out from the pink. "Oh, Toby!" she
exclaimed. "Your first tooth!" She bent down to
look at it and he beamed obligingly, as if showing
it off.

Molly couldn't help thinking about the shark's
teeth she'd seen with Delphi. She was glad her
baby brother's teeth weren't quite so sharp!

"Isn't it a beautiful morning?" Molly's gran said just then, coming into the room slowly, leaning on her cane. "I can't believe it, when it was so stormy last night. The clouds have melted away as if by magic."

Molly grinned at her gran while her mom's back was turned. "As if by magic," she echoed, and winked.

Then she settled down to her breakfast with a smile on her face. A day on the beach today, and another mermaid adventure to look forward to soon... She truly felt like the luckiest girl in the world.

The End

For more magical
underwater adventures visit
www.edcpub.com
or
www.usbornebooksandmore.com

To find out more
about Molly and all her
mermaid friends, and have
some magical ocean fun,
check out

www.secret-mermaid.com

Sue Mongredien has published over 60 books, including the magical *Oliver Moon, Junior Wizard* series. Like Molly Holmes, Sue loves exploring, and gave up a job as an editor of children's books to travel the world, before becoming a full-time writer. Sue also loves the sea, and had a house near Brighton beach in England before moving to Bath, also in England, where she now lives with her husband and three children.

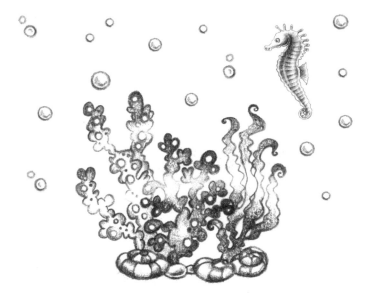

If you've enjoyed **The Secret Mermaid**,
you might also enjoy:

Amy Wild, Animal Talker

by Diana Kimpton

Welcome to the world of Amy Wild, where
dogs tell their secrets, cats perform rescue
missions, and an entire island is squeaking
and squawking with animal magic!

Animal lovers everywhere will be
instantly enchanted by this Dr. Dolittle
for a new generation.

The Pony-Crazed Princess

by Diana Kimpton

Princess Ellie is crazy about horses!
And she's fed up with being a princess!
She hates frilly pink dresses, and boring
waving lessons. She'd much rather be
riding one of her four gorgeous ponies!